The Valiant
Chatti-maker

The Valiant Chatti-maker

Rumer Godden
illustrated by Jeroo Roy

The Viking Press
New York

NOTE

Based on a version by Sir Owain Jenkins,
to whose knowledge and wit this story
is deeply indebted.

First American Edition

Text Copyright © Rumer Godden 1983
Illustrations Copyright © Jeroo Roy 1983

Published in 1983 by The Viking Press
40 West 23rd Street, New York, New York 10010

Printed in Hong Kong

1   2   3   4   5   87   86   85   84   83

Library of Congress Cataloging in Publication Data

Godden, Rumer, 1907-
The valiant chatti maker.

Summary: When he inadvertently captures the tiger that
has been terrorizing the neighborhood, a poor potter not
only gains fame and fortune but the unwanted honor of
leading the Raja's army against an invading enemy.
[1. India – Fiction.   2. Humorous stories]   I. Roy,
Jeroo, ill.   II. Title.
PZ7. G54Val   1983   [Fic]   83-7000

ISBN 0-670-74236-8

This is an old story. It used to be told by an Ayah, an Indian nurse-maid, to the children she looked after. The Ayah knew it by heart and had told it so often that it came out exactly word for word as if she were wound up. If anyone interrupted her she had to go back to the beginning and start again. The children never minded.

Once upon a time, in India, there lived a poor Chatti-Maker. Chattis are earthenware pots; huge ones for storing grain and rice, middle sized ones for carrying water – the women filled them at the well and carried them home balanced on their heads – all sizes of pots down to the tiny bowls called kullars used in the tea-stalls and toddy shops. The Chatti-Maker shaped each one carefully with his hands and fingers as the heavy wooden wheel spun; he set them to dry in the sun outside the shed built onto his house, then baked them in the kiln in his small yard until each pot was golden-red, the colour of ripe apricots.

His house and work-shed were in the workman's village outside the City walls. The City was built on a hill with a river at the bottom; at the top of the hill the Raja lived in a pink marble palace with his ladies; there were a great many of them, besides courtiers and soldiers, servants, peacocks and pigeons, horses and elephants.

Below the Raja's palace was the temple and the houses of the Priests or Brahmins who were extremely holy and extremely particular.

Below the Brahmins lived the Rajputs, warriors, fierce proud men who wore enormous turbans and had great whiskers and moustaches.

Below the Rajputs were the Bunnias, shopkeepers and bankers. They wore little round hats, were fat as butter and very cunning.

Outside the walls and beyond the Chatti-Maker's village, other villages spread away among crops and fields where the country

people lived and worked. It all belonged to the Raja. If anybody met him, they had to step off the road and lie face downwards in the dust till he had passed; if anyone displeased him, it was his right to send for his head elephant – its name was Asoka – to come and trample them and squash them flat, but this Raja preferred not to think of uncomfortable things like being squashed flat and so far no-one had been trampled in his reign.

However, "Just to remind people", said the Raja, every evening he sent Asoka swaying down through the City to the river for his evening bath and everyone saw the elephant's mighty tusks, the tassels of honour that hung beside his ears, and above all his huge feet. "It keeps my people meek and obedient", said the Raja, which meant they did not trouble him and he could play games, go on picnics, watch dancing girls and listen to music in peace.

This was all very well for those who lived behind the City walls, but for the people outside it was different. The Chatti-Maker and the tailors and tinkers and carpenters worked from morning till night, as did the villagers, added to which a Tiger had begun to maraud around them. He was an enormous Tiger with splendid stripes and whiskers larger than the Raja's; he was lazy and found it easier to prey round the villages than to hunt in the jungle – deer run so fast – and every other night he would take a cow or a calf, even a bullock for his dinner. "If we shut the cattle up soon he'll be taking one of us", said the villagers. "Aie! Aie! Our babies!" shrilled the wives.

The village Headman went to the Raja and asked him to come and shoot the Tiger. "If you come on Asoka you will be perfectly safe", they told him but, "Presently, presently", said the Raja. "I have pressing business" – he was going to practice archery with his Princesses, and beside he had no idea where his gun was. He meant to go and look for it but kept putting it off.

The Headmen went to the Brahmins but they turned up their eyes in horror. "It is forbidden to take life."

"The Tiger takes it all the time."
"Forbid it to."

"If you would come and forbid it, Holy Ones", but the Brahmins said their place was in the temple.

The Rajputs were playing chess. "Let us finish our game", they said, "and we'll come with our swords", but one game led to another – besides their swords were rusty.

"*You* can make the Raja do anything, because you have all his money", the Headmen told the Bunnias. "Remind him of that."

"We'll remind him tomorrow", said the Bunnias, but the Raja might have taken his money away from them and they preferred to keep the money.

The Chatti-Maker had not heard about the Tiger – he kept himself
to himself. He had to. Though he worked hard making his chattis
as beautifully as he knew how and when, once a week he loaded
up his Donkey to sell them in the City and villages, he sold every
one, he was still poor because no-one paid him the proper price.

"The clay belongs to the Raja", said the Palace servants and
took them for nothing.

The Brahmins said the chattis were a gift to the temple and paid
nothing either.

The Rajputs were too proud to count; they threw the Chatti-
Maker coins and said, "Keep the change", but, as they threw too
few, there was never any change.

The Bunnias said the pots were lopsided, the wrong colour, or
cracked and only paid half price.

The village people paid what they could; the Chatti-Maker had
not the heart to ask for more, and besides he was too modest to
argue.

His only good customer was the toddy shop for whom he made
the tiny kullars. The toddy shop used a great many because it is
an Indian custom that, when a kullar has been drunk from, it is
immediately smashed; the Shop Keeper, though, did not pay the
Chatti-Maker in money but let him have as much toddy as he
could swallow, so every evening he loaded up his Donkey with
kullars and, taking his staff, which had belonged to his father,
grandfather and great-grandfather, went to the shop. Toddy is
made of the fermented juice of palm trees and tastes like beer but
is much, much stronger and when the Chatti-Maker had had
three or four kullars he forgot how poor he was and felt, not only
as good as the next man, but as if he were the Raja himself.

In the morning he was a poor humble Chatti-Maker again.

In that part of India, except for pink marble palaces, houses and
temples were built of black stone with red tiled roofs, though

there were a few mud-walled thatched huts. Every house had its courtyard, hedged with cactus which was prickly and had red flowers and, in each courtyard, there was a plant of 'tulsi' or basil, which is not only sweet to smell and good to eat but sacred and so brings luck.

In the Chatti-Maker's courtyard there were only chattis drying; he had no tulsi plant. "Perhaps that's why I'm so poor", he said and asked as he had asked a thousand times, "What am I to do? What can I do?"

"Plant a tulsi, ek dum", said his Clever Little Wife – 'ek dum' means 'at once'.

For a long time the Chatti-Maker had not had a wife; no father

13

would let his daughter marry him because he was so poor, but the Clever Little Wife had been a different kind of daughter. One day, when she had come down to the river to do her washing – she beat the clothes on the river's flat stones – she had seen the Chatti-Maker digging his clay. Though he was not handsome, having a dark skin and a back bent from sitting over his wheel, she noticed his hands, which were big and strong, and noticed as well how gentle they were when the moved a pai-dog puppy that wanted to dig clay too, out of the way; noticed how children followed him home – he made them little horses and dolls out of spare pieces of clay – and she went to her father and told him he must marry her to the Chatti-Maker, "Ek dum". When she said 'Ek dum' it always seemed to happen and, as this story begins, the lucky marriage garlands of mango leaves still hung green around the Chatti-Maker's house as he and his new Little Wife planted a tulsi in their courtyard.

The Clever Little Wife came with him when he went out to sell his chattis, walking behind him and the Donkey as an Indian wife should but, though she kept the end of her sari modestly across her face, she whispered to the Chatti-Maker what he should say.

"Tell the palace servants to inform the Raja that you know the clay is his, but *he* hasn't dug it and turned it into something useful."

"True", said the Raja who was always fair-minded, and he ordered his servants to pay the proper price.

"Tell the Brahmins a gift is not gifts. One chatti for the temple, no more", and the Brahmins had to pay for the rest.

As for the Rajputs – "You must teach them the twice times table", said the Clever Little Wife. The twice times was enough because chattis are cheap. "And when they say, twice two are four, you say, twice four are eight." The Rajputs were amused at the Chatti-Maker's quickness and gave him the full eight.

14

"Your pots are not in the least lopsided and a good colour. Not one is cracked. Listen", and she made them go 'ping' with her fingernail to prove it. "Tell the Bunnias if they won't pay for them you'll take them away, ek dum", and the Bunnias paid.

In those days people had to have chattis; there was nothing else in which to carry water or store grain, and soon everyone was paying the proper price. "See. It's our tulsi", she said, but the Chatti-Maker knew it was she, the Clever Little Wife.

She worked all day as a potter's wife should, carrying the clay in an iron pan on her head, helping to mix it with water until it was slimy and wet so that he could take a lump and spin it on his wheel; then she would gather wood to make the fire in the kiln and help to stoke it. By evening she was tired and dirty but she always washed, put on a clean sari and a little bodice called a 'choli' that left her waist cool and bare. She would brush and oil her hair and plait a jasmine or frangi-pani flower into it.

The Chatti-Maker now had his dinner served to him on a brass tray, polished; it was only chapattis and a pillau, a rice dish; the Little Wife had nothing to go with the rice except sāg, a kind of wild spinach that can be had for the picking and what herbs she had been able to find – but to him it tasted delicious. She herself afterwards ate what the Chatti-Maker had left – though he was hungry he was careful to leave enough. Then he would take the Donkey and the kullars and leave for the toddy shop.

The Clever Little Wife did not mind: she had the dishes to wash, the floor to sweep, which she did with a little broom of stiff grass; sometimes to amuse herself she would make a pattern on the floor with millet seeds and a paste of white ashes from the stove. Last thing, she lit a tiny earthenware lamp – it had a wick in oil – and set it below the tulsi bush and said a prayer. "Please, Sitala" – Sitala is the name of a Goddess who is particularly kind to Potters. "Please, Sitala, we are doing quite well but, please, make us a little less poor, so we can have milk and butter on our chapattis and some spices to flavour our pillaus" – she did not presume to ask for meat – "and please, please, a little less sāg." As the Clever Little Wife prayed with the light on her face, her hands joined in reverence, the Chatti-Maker, coming back from the toddy shop, thought he had never seen anyone as beautiful.

One night, though, he did not come back in time to see her, nor could she light the lamp because there was a stupendous, tremendous storm.

It began with clouds gathering dark and low. Then the wind got up, so fierce a wind that the palm tree leaves rustled and beat, and the banner outside the village's own temple was whipped off its tall bamboo pole. There was a roll of thunder, a clap so loud that cocks and hens and goats went scurrying; the people shouted and ran to call in their children and tie up their animals more safely, or bring them into the house, as more thunder rolled with lightning. The whole sky went crack-rumble-rumble-crack.

Opposite the Chatti-Maker's house was a hut where an old Widow lived. The hut's walls were tumbledown, its thatched roof full of holes, its courtyard dirty. At first the villagers had been sorry for this Widow – in India widows do not often live alone – but soon they learned that she had lived with her son and quarrelled with him, then with her second son and quarrelled with him, then with her daughter, her nephew, niece, cousins, and cousin's cousins and quarrelled with them all. She did nothing but quarrel and shout abuse and, in her dirty white sari, with her shaven head, she was so wrinkled and brown it seemed she had been pickled in malice and spite. She had no teeth but her words were sharp enough to bite and she was so disagreeable that soon no-one came near her but, as the storm grew fiercer, the Chatti-Maker's Little Wife thought she must go over and ask the Widow to come and take shelter with her.

"With *you*! No thank *you*", spat the Widow. "Aie! Haven't I watched you in your scarlet choli, you hussy! Flowers in your hair and all that brushing! And still that good-for-nothing husband of yours goes off to the toddy shop. He's there now, isn't he?" the old Widow cackled with glee. "Isn't he? Isn't he?"

"I hope he is", said the Clever Little Wife, "then he'll be safe and warm", and she went back home and, being like all sensible people afraid of thunder, went to bed and put the quilt over her head so that she heard nothing more.

The thunder and lightning went crack-rumble-rumble and soon with a loud hissing, the rain came down in torrents. In no time at all it had leaked through the holes in the Widow's thatch, going 'drip, drip' on the bed and cupboard and onto the floor and 'ring, ting, ting' on the pans on the stove, 'hiss-sss' on the fire. The Widow began to move things about to avoid the wet places

17

but the more she moved them the wetter they got and she began to shout and curse. "This perpetual dripping!" she yelled. "It'll be the death of me", and, "I'd rather deal with a lion or a rhinoceros than this perpetual dripping."

At that moment the Tiger came by.

The Headmen had gone to the Raja again and again. Last time, "bring *all* your elephants", they had begged. "but come."

"The elephants are not available", the Raja had said "They have taken the palace ladies for a 'hawa-khana' – which means 'to eat the air', in other words for an airing. "I'll come by and by", which the Headmen had known meant never and, they asked in despair, "Who will rid us of this terrible Tiger?"

The Tiger was not at all terrible now. He had come out to catch his dinner – his whiskers had alerted him to a particularly toothsome plump heifer calf – but the storm had caught him instead and he was soaked to his last stripe; his whiskers were sodden, his tail between his legs. He was even more afraid of thunder than the Chatti-Maker's wife and every time he heard crack, rumble, crack, he cowered. There must be an Ogre in the sky, he thought. Then he saw that the thatch of the Widow's hut hung down in eaves making a dark small shelter each side, dry because there the thatch was thick. It was the very place for a frightened Tiger and he crept in, lying close to the wall, and in a minute he was more frightened still.

Hunting so close to the villagers, he had come to understand human talk and now he heard the Widow's shoutings.

"Rather a lion or rhinoceros than this perpetual dripping. Worse than a rhinoceros", she shouted.

18

"Worse than a rhinoceros!" The Tiger quailed. "This Perpetual Dripping must be the Ogre in the sky."

"Rather a mad elephant or a thousand horsemen than this perpetual dripping", the Widow broke out again and 'bang' went a saucepan, then a frying pan. "This perpetual dripping has got my very bones", yelled the Widow and the Tiger made himself as small as possible for fear Perpetual Dripping would come and get his bones as well.

At last the Widow knew she had to go for help. "Even from that hussy", and she opened the hut door. Before she could close it, the wind swirled in, blew out the folds of her sari and took her out of the hut and up into the sky. She was thin and dry, light as a leaf and it whirled her high over the village, round and round until she was senseless, then impaled her on the spike of the village temple's bamboo pole, and that was the end of the widow.

The Tiger had heard her shriek. Perpetual Dripping has taken her for his dinner, he thought – he knew no other way of dying – and he'll come back and eat me too! He crouched lower and shut his eyes tight.

Meanwhile the Donkey, who had been tied outside the toddy shop but with no toddy inside him to make him brave, was just as frightened by the storm as was the Tiger. He brayed and kicked and squealed, tugging at his rope and halter. No-one heard him but, when a particularly loud crack of lightning came, he broke his halter strap and galloped off home as fast as his hooves could carry him.

The Chatti-Maker usually tethered him between two palm trees with a pile of grass cut fresh, a chatti of water and the Donkey would stay obediently there, but now the rain was flailing down and he, too, knew of the dry places under the eaves of the Widow's hut. Sometimes he tried to shelter there in the monsoon, the rainy season, until she chased him out with shouts and curses. Tonight the Donkey thought the hut was oddly silent but, still, he walked on the tips of his hooves as he went in – fortunately for him he chose the empty eave. He leaned against the hut wall and went to sleep.

After three or four kullars of toddy the Chatti-Maker got up to go home but, "You can't go home in this", said the Shop Keeper. "It would be dangerous", so the Chatti-Maker stayed and drank three or four more kullars, then five or six. Soon there was no toddy left but, by that time the Chatti-Maker felt, not just like the Raja, but a dozen Rajas and, "I *will* go home", he said.

"But, the storm?"

"I shall tell it to stop", and when the Chatti-Maker came out of the shop he shook his staff at the sky and shouted, "Stop it! Be quiet!" The sky, of course, took not the slightest notice: the thunder still crashed and the rain came down as hard as ever, which put the Chatti-Maker into a fearful rage – as the staff had belonged to his father, grandfather and great-grandfather, the sky should have been more respectful.

20

He was in a worse rage when he could not find his Donkey – he had meant to sit on the Donkey and let him find the way home. "*Shaitan!*" shouted the Chatti-Maker, which means Satan. "Nitwit!! Rascal. Gone off and left me, have you? Thought you'd run home? I'll beat the hide off you. Wait till I catch you. I'll dust your jacket for you."

He took the rope and broken halter and, cursing, stumbling, drenched, made his way home. No Donkey stood between the trees but the Chatti-Maker guessed where he had gone and there, sure enough, under one of the Widow's hut eaves, a flash of lightning showed him what he thought was a familiar shape. "Aha!" shouted the Chatti-Maker. "You think you're going to spend the night there, snug and dry. I'll show you." The Tiger, because of course it was the Tiger, was too frightened to roar. Between the thunder and the Chatti-Maker's shouts he was sure this was Perpetual Dripping come to fetch him, more sure when the Chatti-Maker gave him a tremendous thump with his staff. Then he seized the Tiger by the ear – he was too full of toddy to notice it was a different sort of ear – and gave him a fierce thrashing, put on the halter – with the strap broken it fitted – and dragged the Tiger out from under the eave.

"You'll spend the night out here in the storm, Shaitan", he shouted and with the donkey's rope tied the Tiger between the palm trees. "Run away, will you?" he thumped the Tiger again and, to make quite sure, used more rope – he kept it for tying his chattis onto the Donkey – and shackled the Tiger on all four feet, lashing him round and round. Then he fetched the net that held the pots, put it over the Tiger's head and pulled it so tight that it flattened his whiskers and he could not have opened his mouth even had he felt like biting; not that he did. He was sure it was a matter of minutes before he would be killed and eaten but the Chatti-Maker only shouted, "That'll teach you", gave him another thump for luck, went into the house and fell into bed where,

21

because of all the toddy, he snored. The snoring made almost as much noise as the storm.

The Clever Little Wife always got up at dawn. Though she would only wear her working clothes, she liked to go down to the river to wash herself and say her prayers, then go to the well to fill her chatti with drinking water before she made the Chatti-Maker's breakfast of chapattis and, she sighed, sāg, but as soon as she opened the house door she stopped. "Aie!" She almost ran back inside because there, where the Donkey should have been fastened between the palms, was a tiger. "Aie!" She rubbed her eyes, but no mistaking; it was a huge, huge tiger tied up. Trembling, she stole out to look but the Tiger was tied head and foot, all four feet, and done up in such a cocoon of ropes that it could not possibly move. "Bahadur!" breathed the Little Wife, which means brave. "My brave Chatti-Maker," but, "He must have drunk a lot of toddy," she said. Even so! "Bahadur! Bara Bahadur, very brave", she said and went to call the neighbours.

They came pell-mell and could not believe their eyes until the Headman pronounced, "It is *that* Tiger."

The Tiger did not feel like *that* Tiger any more. He was so ashamed of his flattened whiskers, so cramped with the ropes, besides thinking that any moment Perpetual Dripping might come and finish him off, that he could only lie still giving most untigerlike whimpers. "Rām! Rām!" the villagers said reverently – Rām is one of the names of God – and at once they and the Clever Little Wife went to tell the Raja how the Chatti-Maker had captured the Tiger that had been the terror of the land. "Single handed", put in the Clever Little Wife, and, "Single handed", echoed the villagers.

"Shabash! Hooray!" said the Raja and ordered, "Put the Tiger in the Royal Zoo."

"And what about my husband?" the Clever Little Wife was quick to ask. "Doesn't he get anything?"

"Indeed he does", said the Raja and called for his Dewan, the Palace Lord Chamberlain, who was also the Raja's Giver of Gifts and Dispenser of Royal Favours, "Make a Procession", ordered the Raja. "With flags and a band. Let the Chatti-Maker be named Valiant, invest him with a Robe of Honour and a Noble Puggaree. Fill his mouth with gold and give him Command of a Thousand Horse."

When the Chatti-Maker woke up, the Tiger had been taken away and the Procession had not started so the village was uncommonly quiet. His Little Wife was not there to serve his breakfast – he did not want any anyway – but he only supposed that everyone was working and she had gone to fetch clay, which made him feel guilty; he had a bad headache, too, which told him he had drunk too much toddy. The Donkey was standing in his usual place, his ears twitching because he was a little afraid. He knew he should not have run away but the Chatti-Maker had forgotten everything that had happened last night and washed his face, rinsed his mouth, put on a clean loin-cloth – he did not

23

wear anything else when he was working – and went to his shed, wet his clay and set about making a chatti.

Presently he began to have a strange ringing in his ears. The ringing noise grew worse every moment until it was more than he could bear. "Tum, tum, tootle, tootle, tum", it went like a brass band and he looked up. There indeed was the Raja's Palace Band marching towards him, led by a splendid nobleman on a horse which was hung about with grand trappings. He was followed by soldiers and a crowd of people, and all the Headmen – the news had spread to the other villages – but who did the Chatti-Maker see behind them all? Asoka!

Asoka was only carrying the Raja who had not been able to resist coming to see, "But not too close", he told his Mahout, the man who drove the elephant. "Not too close, my dear fellow. It doesn't do to seem too interested." All the same, when the Chatti-Maker saw Asoka, he was so frightened that sweat trickled down his back and legs, though he could not think of anything he had done that deserved being squashed flat. He was more frightened still when two soldiers came and seized him. His hands were wet and slimy with clay and, "You'll get it on your uniforms", he cried in dismay. "At least let me wash my hands." They would not listen but marched him out of the courtyard.

"Oh! Rāma, save me", prayed the Chatti-Maker. "Save me." Then in the crowd he saw his Little Wife. She was nodding and smiling and suddenly he felt better.

The Dewan, Giver of Gifts and Dispenser of Royal Favours, got down from his horse, called for a table and put down on it a bowl full of gold mohurs, large heavy coins squiggled with the Raja's name. The drums rolled a salute, the trumpeters blew a fanfare, the two soldiers brought the Chatti-Maker to the table and the Dewan, who was exceedingly pompous, began, "Behold our Chatti-Maker, who alone and single handed, has captured and bound this most ferocious and man-eating tiger" – the Tiger, to give him his due, had never even tasted man, woman, or child but, "this man-eating Tiger", chanted the Dewan.

The Chatti-Maker was aghast. "That was nothing . . ." he said. He had meant to finish, " . . . nothing to do with me", but his words were drowned in a roar of admiration. "Did you hear him?" the people asked one another. "*Nothing* to capture a tiger!" and the Dewan beamed grandly as he went on. "Oh, Chatti-Maker! By Order of His Exalted Highness, you are to be named Valiant. You will be given Command of a Thousand Horse, invested with a Robe of Honour and a Noble Puggaree and your mouth is to be filled with gold. We shall begin with last. Open your mouth", and, with his fingers carefully crooked to keep them from touching the Chatti-Maker's mouth, the Dewan dropped the first gold mohur on his tongue.

"I don't like the taste", spluttered the Chatti-Maker, but the Clever Little Wife had darted forward. "Open your mouth *wide*," she told him and, "Proceed", she said to the soldiers, "but not too fast. I don't want him to choke", and so, using a piece of wood shaped like a shoehorn, they slid coin after coin into the Chatti-Maker's mouth. Clonk, clonk, clonk, each went against his teeth – it was like posting letters – clonk, clonk. The Chatti-Makers's mouth got fuller and fuller, he could not breath but, just as he thought he must swallow the coins and die, the Dewan said, "Stop."

"Put them out. Put them out", cried the Clever Little Wife holding out the end of her sari to catch them. A soldier thumped the Chatti-Maker on the back and the coins came pouring out, more money than he or his Little Wife had seen in all their lives. The villagers laughed and cheered, and this was not all.

The Dewan called an attendant who brought a big bag of money. "Behold the pay for the Thousand Horse of which you are in Command", said the Dewan.

Then the attendants brought a magnificent Robe of Honour embroidered with gold and diamonds and put it on the Chatti-Maker. On his head they wound a saffron coloured Puggaree or turban of the finest muslin, arranged in knots and curliques, one end floating down behind; the turban made his head look twice its proper size so that it was no surprise when the Dewan announced, "You are now called The Valiant and the Leader of One Thousand Horse. Every year you will receive a royal bag of gold." Then he took the gold mohurs that were left in the bowl and some out of the bag and put them in his purse which he always carried with him. "This is my dastoori – the luck-money you give me."

"I didn't give it, you took it!" the Chatti-Maker, who was incurably honest, had to say, but, "Hush! It is the custom", whispered the Clever Little Wife. The brass band blew their trumpets and beat their drums, striking up a march – Asoka and the Raja had discreetly disappeared. The Dewan, Giver of Gifts and Dispenser of Royal Favours, mounted his horse and all of them marched away to the palace, leaving the Chatti-Maker utterly bewildered and with his headache worse than ever. "Please take off this turban", he begged his Little Wife.

She was not at all bewildered. "Indeed I will", she said, "and that robe too, before it gets dirty. They must be kept for best", and she put them away in the cupboard which she locked; the key was tied in the corner of her sari. "Can I go back to the chatti I was making?' the Chatti-Maker asked her. "Aie! The clay will have dried out now."

She let him go but, that night, she made a feast, a pillau, not only with spices, chilli and saffron but fat pieces of goat meat as well and not a trace of sāg. The pillau was followed by sweetmeats and she even fetched some toddy; she paid for it in kullars but bought a little sherbet for herself.

The Brahmins came to the Chatti-Maker. "With all that gold, the Gods feel you should make an offering to the temple."

The Chatti-Maker did not answer, but went on spinning his wheel.

The Rajputs came. "With all that gold, couldn't you lend us a handful or two, dear chap, and we'll teach you to play chess."

The Chatti-Maker went on spinning his wheel.

The Bunnias came to him, one by one. "With all that gold, I feel you should put it in my bank, but don't tell the others."

The Chatti-Maker went on spinning his wheel.

When they had all gone, he sent for the goldsmith and had him make a gold necklace for his Clever Little Wife, gold bracelets for her wrists, a gold ring for each ear and a pretty little gold ring for her nose. The rest of the money he put back in its bag and hid it under his bed in a tin trunk painted with roses; then he went back to making chattis. The sound of his wheel was soothing after all the upset but sometimes, in the days that followed, he stopped the wheel and sat still to wonder. "Did I really do that to the Tiger?" he asked. He who did not want to hurt anyone, not even a man-eating tiger.

As a matter of fact the Tiger was much relieved. In the Zoo the bars of his cage were so strong that he knew Perpetual Dripping, of whom he was still mortally afraid, could not get at him; besides he was given two dinners every day without having to hunt and could spend his days lying in the sun, his stomach pleasantly filled.

That too was the chief difference in the Chatti-Maker's life; having more money the Clever Little Wife made better and better food. Every evening when she took her lamp to the tulsi bush she would say, "Thank you, Sitala." Another difference was that the

Chatti-Maker grew a moustache and a pair of whiskers almost as splendid as the Raja's or the Tiger's; the village barber came to oil and curl them every day.

Only one bother disturbed the Chatti-Maker, a bother that grew to a trouble. On the first day of the first month every year, the Dewan, Giver of Gifts and Dispenser of Royal Favours called but without the band of soldiers, and brought the Chatti-Maker another bag of money, pay for the Commander of a Thousand Horse. The Dewan always took his dastoori-luck-money.

This reminded the Chatti-Maker that he ought not to put the bags under his bed – he had had to buy another tin trunk – but use the money to buy horses and recruit men, arming them and drilling them.

"The Dewan didn't *tell* you to do that", pointed out the Clever Little Wife.

"It goes without saying", said the Chatti-Maker gloomily. "The Commander of a Thousand Horse should have a thousand horse and I haven't."

"How could you get them?" she asked.

"I haven't the slightest idea, besides", and he cheered up a little, "if I go about recruiting and buying horses, what will people do for their chattis? Surely chattis are more important."

"Well then", said the Little Wife.

"Is it well?" Again he was troubled. "If the Raja hears he'll certainly send Asoka to squash me."

"Asoka is an elephant. Elephants don't squash their friends", she said, but, just to make sure, the Clever Little Wife made the Chatti-Maker waylay Asoka on the way to the river and give him sugar cane and a sticky yellow sweet called halwa and, every year, the Chatti-Maker went back to his chattis for another year.

A Messenger, out of breath with running, appeared in the palace where the Raja was playing chess with his favourite Page.

"Exalted Highness", panted the Messenger. "The Northern Raja has invaded your Kingdom. He is encamped in the Waterless Desert with a vast army and says he will put our City to sword and fire."

"Tut! Tut!" said the Raja. "Your move, my boy", he said to the Page. Then to the Messenger, "Send for the Commander-in-Chief."

The Commander-in-Chief was playing chess too. He was so dismayed that he upset the chess-board. "Rām! Rām!" he wailed, and "We must make terms", he told the Raja. "We are outnumbered. Make terms", begged the Commander-in-Chief.

"Nonsense", said the Raja. Then, "Never."

"But, Your Highness, I haven't a man who has fired a musket for the last five years. The only uniforms they have are dress uniforms."

"Why?" thundered the Raja.

"It's been so pleasurable living in your Majesty's Kingdom. We . . . we never thought of war."

"You had better think now," but, "Too late!" the Commander-in-Chief wept. "We shall have to surrender."

The Raja's father would have called for Asoka at once but this Raja knew it was partly his fault for making his kingdom so pleasurable and he only said, "Nonsense", again, and walked to and fro pulling his moustache – though, it must be owned, he would have liked to pull the Commander-in-Chief's moustache too. That miserable person had knelt down, taken off his turban and put it at the Raja's feet, a sign of abject subjection. "Do get up", the Raja said testily, and then, "This needs", he said, "a Commander of Valour and Decision. Not like *you*", he said ignoring the turban and, suddenly, "like that fellow who caught the Tiger all by himself. He and his Thousand Horse should settle the question. Send a herald to tell him to go to the Waterless Desert at once."

The Herald, on his horse, trotted swiftly through the City. "What's the hurry?" the people shouted, and the Herald shouted back over his shoulder, "Invasion", and the news spread.

The Brahmins ran to the temple and beat gongs and blew conch shells, "Ulla-ulla-loo."

The Rajputs shouted their war cries and tried to remember where they had put their swords.

The Bunnias began packing and putting their money in bags ready to run away.

The villagers began to round up their cattle but, because of the whirr of his wheel, the Chatti-Maker heard nothing until the Herald came to the house and blew his trumpet.

The Chatti-Maker thought it was the Donkey braying and paid no attention but the Clever Little Wife darted out. Then, "Come", she called to him. "Come at once."

"But it isn't the first day of the first month", protested the Chatti-Maker.

"Listen", said his Little Wife. "This gentleman has something to tell you."

The Herald blew his trumpet again. He was even more pompous than the Dewan. "Go forth", he cried, "Go forth, O Valiant Leader of a Thousand Horse, and vanquish the Enemy Army in the Waterless Desert."

"What?" cried the Chatti-Maker.

"You heard", said the Herald. "By Order of his Exalted Highness the Raja."

"Wife! Wife! What am I to do?" The Chatti-Maker had drawn her back into the house. "Now they'll find out I haven't one horse, let alone a thousand. I haven't any men. The Raja! Asoka! The Raja! Wife! Wife! What am I to do?" and the Clever Little Wife answered at once, "First ask leave to reconnoitre the position."

35

The Chatti-Maker came out and said to the Herald, "Ask his Exalted Highness if I may first go alone to reconnoitre the position and find out the strength of the enemy before I deploy my horses."

"Excellent!" said the Raja. "This fellow is as wise as he is courageous. Let him have the best horse in my stable."

No sooner had the Herald left, tnan the Little Wife acted swiftly. "Get out your Donkey", she said, "and here, take your lota" – his brass drinking pot; she tied a few handfuls of parched grain in the tail of his turban. "Once among the crops", she said, "among the tall millet and high sugar cane, who can tell which way you go. Once outside the Kingdom who will notice a poor potter on his donkey? So, make for the border and I will join you with the money as soon as I can.' Then she thought and said, "But first I must cut off your moustache and whiskers."

"No! *No!*" the Chatti-Maker clapped his hands over them. "You can't."

"I must. They don't become a poor potter." She fetched the scissors which she kept locked in the cupboard wrapped in a silk handkerchief – no-one else in the village had a pair of scissors – but before she could use them there was a great noise of stamping and champing in the courtyard, a clinking of chains, of the sound of men cursing, and there was the Herald again. With him was an enormous black horse wearing a rich saddle and jewelled bridle and reins. He was snorting and kicking at the grooms who were trying to hold him.

'The Raja has sent you his best horse to ride on your mission", said the Herald. "It's name is Bijli – Lightning. You'll find out why." He blew a blast on his trumpet that made Bijli rear, then rode away laughing to the palace.

"Aie! Aie!" the Chatti-Maker could not help his teeth chattering and his knees shaking as he cried, "I'm as good as dead." The Clever Little Wife, though, stayed calm and beckoned the Chatti-Maker into the house. "We must change our plan", she said. "But if we keep a high hand I think we can still carry it off."

"I haven't got a high hand", moaned the Chatti-Maker, but the Little Wife had already gone to the cupboard. She put the scissors away and took out the Robe of Honour in which she dressed the Chatti-Maker and tied the great saffron Puggaree with its knots and curliques and long floating end, on his head. She put a whip in one hand and fetched a bag of money from the tin trunk to put in the other. "Now", she said and took him back outside . "Mount the horse and ride openly along the road. To those who salaam throw a coin. Those who don't, give a lash of your whip and everyone will think you are a nobleman, and you can ride safely to the Border."

"Safely", the Chatti-Maker almost shrilled. "How can I ride that great brute? I have never ridden anything except my Donkey. I can't."

"You must. The Raja sent him", and she said, "We'll tie you to the saddle."

"How do I get up to it?" asked the Chatti-Maker. "The saddle is higher than my head."

"Jump", said the Clever Little Wife.

"Jump", said the grooms.

The Chatti-Maker tried but each time Bijli shied away.

"Jump", cried the wife.

"Jump", shouted the grooms, trying to hold the horse still, "Ari! *Jump.*"

The Chatti-Maker gave a mighty leap and landed in the saddle. The grooms and the Little Wife quickly tied the stirrups to his feet and lashed him in the saddle as firmly as he had lashed the Tiger; his hands, into which she put the whip and the money bag, they left free.

All this knotting and lashing of ropes had fidgetted and tickled Bijli beyond bearing and, as the last knot was tied, he broke from his grooms with a snort and at once sprang into a gallop. Gallop, gallop, gallop, through the village, into the City, and out of it again, through its bazaar. Gallop, gallop, gallop. The wind whistled in the Chatti-Maker's ears. He was shaken and bumped. There was no time to see if people salaamed or not; he only knew they screamed and scattered like frightened chickens. Gallop, gallop, gallop, and he and Bijli were in the countryside among the crops, crashing through the tall millet and high sugar cane.

The Chatti-Maker had lost his whip and his bag of money and was clinging with both hands to Bijli's reins and mane. "Stop! Stop!" he cried out but, the more he shouted, the faster Bijli went and, in no time, they had left the millet and sugar cane and were trampling wheat and barley, blue linseed and yellow mustard, and soon the Chatti-Maker knew they were not heading for the Border but for the Waterless Desert and the Invading Army.

"Stop! Stop!"

Gallop, gallop, gallop.

A flight of hornbills flew up – those strange birds with long black beaks and a casque of bone like a helmet that made them look like bird soldiers. They gave cries of warning. "Clatter. Clack. Danger. Danger. Danger. Clatter-clack. Clatter-clack. Danger ahead."

"I know", cried the Chatti-Maker, and to Bijli, "Stop! Stop!" but Bijli crashed into a jungle of babul trees whose thorns scratched and tore the skirts of the Robe of Honour into tatters. Their pricks drew blood on Bijli's flanks but only made him go faster.

Among the babul trees were peacocks in all their brilliant blue and emerald plumage. The Chatti-Maker should have salaamed them – in India peacocks are sacred – but he did not dare let go of Bijli's reins and mane. "Forgive me", he cried but Bijli had startled them up into the highest branches of the babul trees and

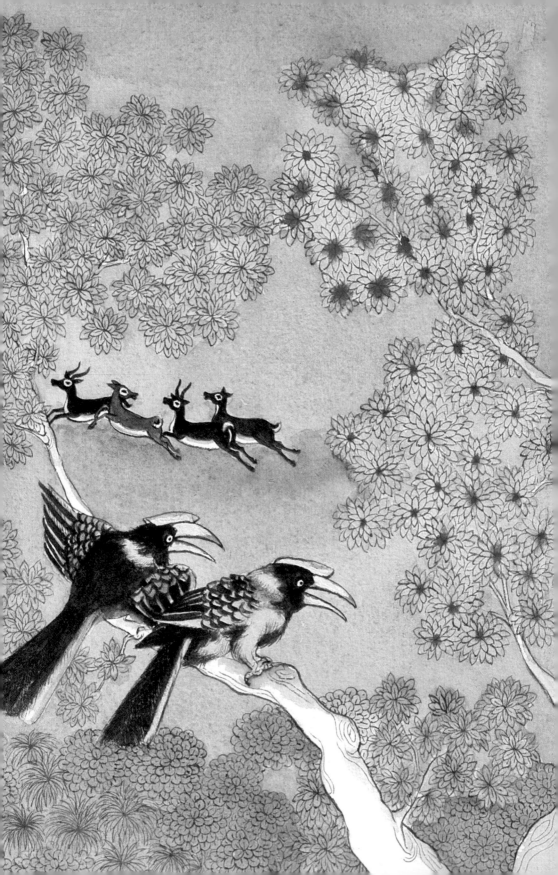

they did not deign to answer. "Meeow! Meeow!" they screeched their cat call as only peacocks can screech and looked angrily at the Chatti-Maker with their little jewelled eyes.

A herd of black buck was grazing, glossy black deer and dun coloured does; hearing the commotion, they raised their heads with their long corkscrew twisted horns, great dark eyes and innocent faces, ready to run, alarmed. Then run they did, galloping too, leaping and raising clouds of dust that got into the Chatti-Maker's nose, making him sneeze and into Bijli's, who gave mighty snorts.

He was galloping now into barren country where only grey-green tamarisks and tufty dry grass and camel thorn grew. Here the wind caught the Chatti-Maker, ballooning out the folds of the Robe of Honour and spreading the tail of his Puggaree so that he looked four times his real size. The gold embroidery glistened in the sun which sent out flashes from the jewels in Bijli's reins and bridle. Bijli's black coat shone, the wind blew out his mane and sent his tail streaming out behind as he galloped faster and faster. The deer ran with them, flying over the tamarisks and thorn bushes. The horn-bills were left behind – they flew too slowly – and, in a moment, the Chatti-Maker could see, across the Waterless Desert, the tents of the Invading Army's Advance Guard and behind them the main encampment. "Stop! Stop! Stop!" he shouted frantically to Bijli. "Danger! Danger! Clack! Clack! Clack!" the hornbills far behind still cried. "Meeow! Meeow! Meeow!" screeched the peacocks in the distance, while the deer's hard little hooves beat a tattoo on the earth that sounded like a hundred small drums rolling.

On the edge of the Desert grew a young banyan tree, that strange tree whose branches send tendrils down into the earth where they root, making a maze of spirals; now, the Chatti-Maker found the strength to loose one hand and grasp the tree, hoping this might stop the great horse in his headlong gallop, but the roots gave way, the banyan's branches and tendrils tangled in the ropes and Bijli galloped on as fast as ever, with the Chatti-Maker dragging the tree and raising an even more gigantic cloud of dust.

In the outposts of the Invading Army's Advance Guard, sentries were on watch. Suddenly one gave a great shout. "Dushman hai – Enemies. Dushman ata – Enemies Advancing."

"How many?" shouted another.

"Thousands. Hear the noise! See the dust they raise!"

"What are they like?"

"I can't see for dust, but huge men on enormous horses. Their clothes glitter. They have I don't know how many attendants, and they are tearing up the trees in their rage."

The Guard Commander came out. "Be quiet, you stupid monkeys! I'm having my supper", he roared, and then, "What's that?" and "Rām!" He began to tremble – the sentries were trembling too.

"What is it they are shouting?" asked the Guard Commander.

"They shout, Stop! Stop! Stop!" said the sentry.

"Not likely," said the Guard Commander and he and the sentries fled towards the tents, loosed their horses, roused the other guards and in a minute the whole Advance Guard was galloping towards the encampment of the Main Army crying, "Giants! Terrible giants. They tear up whole trees in their rage. Fly! Fly! Fly!"

When the Chatti-Maker saw the Advance Guard running away he was so astonished he dropped the tree; at the same time, Bijli, the Lightning, was beginning to slow down and when they reached the tents and he saw the piles of forage and, particularly, the buckets of water for the Enemy Horses' evening feed, he stopped, gave a whinny, trotted to the buckets and drank and drank and drank. The Chatti-Maker took the chance to undo the knots and free himself from the saddle; he slipped down stiff and sore and led Bijli, or rather, Bijli led him to the forage. There the Chatti-Maker tied him to the tent pole and hobbled off to explore.

He did not go far because a wonderfully savoury smell was coming from the Advance Commander's tent where a table was set for supper. The Chatti-Maker sat down and ate until he thought he would burst; he washed the food down with two or three flagons of ruby red wine. "Not as nice as toddy", he said aloud, "but it'll do at a pinch." It had, though, the same effect and, after a while, he began to feel as brave as he had been on the night of the thunderstorm and the Tiger. He even hoped the Enemy would come back. "I'll show them", he yelled. "Let them all come."

In his hurry the Advance Guard Commander had left behind his tulwar, a great curved sword like a scimitar, and the Chatti-Maker began to wave it about. The tulwar felt strange after his wooden staff but it made a fine whistling noise and Smash! Bang! Whang! Whang! he began to break up the dishes on the table. Smash! Bang! Whang! Whang! Now it was the furniture and all the time he roared and shouted and yelled, "Let them all come. I'll dust their jackets for them. I'll make mincemeat of them. I'll . . . I'll . . ."

In the main encampment the Invading Raja was hastily conferring with his Invading Generals.

"Retreat", begged one, his teeth chattering.

"Our men won't stand against people of such enormous stature", said another.

'P-probably their armies are c-close behind them", another looked over his shoulder.

"They tear up trees in their anger!"

"You're cowards", said the Invading Raja. "Poltroons."

"Exalted Highness", they quavered, "we may not contradict your esteemed opinion but. . . ."

"But?" The Invading Raja was fierce.

"If you order your Army to attack they won't obey you, so it's better not to order them", and the oldest Invading General said, "Who can blame them? Listen."

On the wind came the Bang, Whang, the defiant shouts and the great roaring voice of the Chatti-Maker, "Let them all come. I'll make them into mincemeat. Dust their jackets!" Smash! Whang! Bang! Bang!

"What savagery!" the Invading Raja could not suppress a shiver. "They must be demons."

A little later the wind brought the sound of the Chatti-Maker's tremendous snoring, also great huffles from the tired-out Bijli. "The slumber of giants!" The Invading Generals were relieved. "Let's go before they wake."

The Chatti-Maker woke next morning with a horrible headache and once again a ringing in his ears, which was quieter this time, the sound of a band playing but strangely muffled. "Here? In the Waterless Desert?" he asked. "It can't be!" He took several swigs of wine and his head felt better, but the band kept on playing, a subdued tum, tum, tootle, tootle tum, as for a regiment on the march. He staggered to the tent's opening and looked out towards what, he remembered now, was the Invading Army's huge encampment and there, to his astonishment, he saw the entire Army, on horse and on foot, elephants and bullocks, marching away until they disappeared over the opposite hill and the tum, tum, tootle, tootle died away in the distance. "Well, I'll be jiggered!" said the Chatti-Maker but he had not time to stand and stare because he heard Bijli stamping and snorting.

Bijli was pulling his rope so the Chatti-Maker hastily gave him more corn and hay and water, then went back into the tent to get his own breakfast; it was while he was munching a beautiful chappati made of the finest wheat flour and butter and drinking some more wine, that he saw a letter on the table.

It was a large important-looking letter, written in red and black ink and gold and sealed with a gold seal. "How did it get there? The Enemy must have come while I slept!" and, "Aie!" cried the Chatti-Maker.

(The Enemy was the smallest and most insignificant person in the Invading Raja's whole entourage, the Boy who carried his hubble-bubble water pipe. The Invading Raja had had to bribe the Boy with sixteen golden mohurs in a silk net purse.

When the Invading Raja's Dewan, the Enemy Giver of Gifts and Dispenser of Royal Favours, gave the gold mohurs to the Boy, the Dewan kept one as his dastoori. The Invading Generals took one each because they had suggested sending him; as there were fifteen Invading Generals, no gold mohurs were left. The Boy was allowed to keep the purse.)

The Chatti-Maker could not read very well but he made out the name of his own Raja at the top of the letter and, in gold, the word 'Peace' at the bottom. "This must be important," he said to himself. "Perhaps I may not have to run away after all", and, when he had finished his chapatti, he put the letter inside his shirt which he was wearing under the tattered dirty Robe of Honour. Then he put on the belt that held the tulwar – it was so long he had to be careful not to let it trip him up. One end of his Noble Puggaree he filled with provisions for himself, and the other end with some corn for Bijli; he knotted both ends securely, laid them across the saddle and set out to walk home, leading Bijli, the Lightning.

Where he had galloped he now trudged. Trudge, trudge, trudge, the Chatti-Maker went across the Waterless Desert. Bijli trudged too; "I didn't know it was so far," said the Chatti-Maker. Bijli felt the same.

Trudge, trudge. They passed the black buck who raised their heads then went on grazing; passed the peacocks; the females pecked for food: the males turned their backs and spread their tails. The faithful hornbills clacked, "Gone! Gone! Clatter. Clack. The Enemy has run away".

"I know", said the Chatti-Maker. Trudge. Trudge. When he came to the high sugar cane and tall millet he was too tired to go further and Bijli's head was drooping, and they stopped beside a watering pool. With the tulwar he cut some sugar cane for Bijli – after all Bijli had been extremely good – he gave him some corn too and tied him to a tree. Then the Chatti-Maker opened his own provisions – the food was still excellent; he drank a flagon of wine, lay down and, using his Puggaree as a pillow, went to sleep. Bijli slept too.

They woke so early that the stars were still out. "Good", said the Chatti-Maker to Bijli. "We can walk through the City and no-one will see us." This they did and arrived at the village and the Chatti-Maker's house just as dawn was breaking, showing the rim of the rising sun. The sky was pink; small birds had begun to sing, parrakeets to squawk, the crows to caw. It was a chorus of welcome. Bijli gave a neigh, the Donkey woke and shook out his ears, the Little Wife came running out and the world was full of gladness.

Bijli was again tied to a tree and the Chatti-Maker showed the Clever Little Wife the letter. "Is it important?" he asked.

The Clever Little Wife gave a squeal of joy. "Indeed it is", she said. "You must take it straight to the Raja."

The Chatti-Maker looked at his tattered robe, at his scratched hands and dusty feet. "I can't go to the palace like this."

"It's just how you must go", said the Clever Little Wife. "To show the toil and moil, the danger you have been through." The Chatti-Maker set out wearing the tulwar and leading Bijli, the Lightning, but, by this time, the news of the Invading Army's retreat had reached the City and the people crowded round crying, "See the Valiant Commander of a Thousand Horse who has defeated the Enemy and saved our Kingdom", and they said to one another, "See how modest he is. He walks on foot!" Nobody knew that, not for a hundred thousand golden mohurs, would the Chatti-Maker have got up on Bijli again.

The Raja was playing hide-and-seek with his ladies. "Just a moment, my dear fellow", he said. "I must just catch that little Maid of Honour who has such delicious dimples", and he added, "Tashrif rakhiye – Please be seated." Few people, even noblemen, were allowed to sit before the Raja and the Chatti-Maker was quite overcome.

When the Raja had caught the Maid of Honour, the Chatti-Maker made him a deep obeisance and presented the letter which offered surrender and apologised for the invasion. It asked the Raja to accept the whole encampment and its equipment as compensation for damage to the Waterless Desert. The letter ended with pleas of friendship and asked for a treaty of eternal peace. "Aha!" said the Raja and clapped the Chatti-Maker on the shoulder. "Well done!" and he immediately made the Chatti-Maker his new Commander-in-Chief. "Instead of that old nit-wit", he said.

He gave the Chatti-Maker a pink marble palace like his own, only smaller, and invested him with another title. 'Inexpressibly Valiant and Terrible' which, up to then, nobody had been allowed to use except the Raja himself. He also offered the Chatti-Maker a hundred dancing girls but the Chatti-Maker said, "No, thank you." He was quite content with his Clever Little Wife.

"Laudable", said the Brahmins.

"Extraordinary", said the Rajputs.

"Silly", said the Bunnias. "A dancing girl can be worth her weight in gold."

The new Commander-in-Chief – otherwise the Chatti-Maker – and his Little Wife settled down in their marble palace. There were no more wars in his lifetime but still the Chatti-Maker was given such a number of medals and ribbons that the Clever Little Wife was kept busy sewing them on to his dozens of Robes of Honour and uniforms. "But when will I wear them?" asked the Chatti-Maker bewildered.

"When you drill and inspect your troops", she told him, but the Chatti-Maker left that to his Generals. He contented himself by seeing that the troops had proper food and plenty of toddy, which made him more than popular. When he took his army on parade he always had his charger led behind him – the charger was Bijli. The people did not know that not for two hundred thousand mohurs would the Chatti-Maker have mounted Bijli again and soon he had another title, "Modest and Inestimable." He had sent for his Donkey but, "You can't appear riding *that*", said the Clever Little Wife. In any case the Donkey did not like his pink marble stall and ran away back to the village.

Sometimes the Chatti-Maker wished he could run away too. He did not really like Orders and Parades any more than he liked the uniforms, and pined for his comfortable old loin-cloth, the feel of the sun on his back and the peaceful whirr of his wheel. The Clever Little Wife would not let him make chattis because she said it would ruin her nice marble floors but, "Wife. Wife," he said, "My father was a Chatti-Maker, my grandfather and great-grandfather. If I can't make chattis I shall die." The Little Wife did not want her dear Chatti-Maker to die and so, "Ek dum!" a shed was built in the garden without any marble where he made bowls and vases. "For presents," she said, "Not for selling" – a Commander-in-Chief could not go round with a Donkey. As he made them in beautiful shapes and colour, glazing them in India's special deep green blue, they quickly became "Treasures of Art," said the Raja. The Chatti-Maker still called them chattis.

The Clever Little Wife was now a great lady and drove about in a carriage with two scarlet domes on top; it was drawn by four trotting bullocks, milk-white with gilded horns. She had so many cupboards in the palace that she had a special servant to carry her keys instead of having only one tied in the corner of her sari – the saris themselves were too gauzy and fine spun for holding keys. She needed at least fifty saris because she gave splendid parties to which the Raja came, riding in state on Asoka.

Now and again the Brahmins came but they brought their own food, their own saucepans, their own cook, and ate apart.

All the Rajputs always came.

The Bunnias would have liked to come but they were not asked.

The Chatti-Maker did not like parties and when his Little Wife gave one she allowed him to slip away. He could not go to the toddy shop, "That wouldn't be becoming for the Commander-in-Chief," she said, so he went to the Zoo and spent the time with the Tiger with whom he got on well and who, after all, was the beginning of his fortune. "The Tiger or the toddy?" asked the Clever Little Wife. The Chatti-Maker preferred not to answer.

He taught the Tiger to play cat's cradle, which the Tiger took pains to learn because he was eternally gratefuly to the Chatti-Maker for saving him from Perpetual Dripping.